MY DAY
WITH
DAD

RAE CRAWFORD

I Like to Read®

HOLIDAY HOUSE • NEW YORK

I am having a day with my dad.
I smell breakfast.

I mix.
Dad flips.

Yum!

We enjoy every bite.

Dad and I clean up.

Pup wants to help.

Oh no!
It is raining.

We still have fun.
We play games.

I lose.

And I win!

"Look!" I say.
"No more rain."

Dad and I ride.
Pup runs.

We fly kites.

We look at clouds.

It is time to go.
I am so sad.

"We will have more fun at home," Dad says.

We race home.

We make mac and
cheese for dinner.

Mom calls while we eat.

We say good night.

I put on my pj's.
We see a funny movie.

Almost time for bed.
What is Dad hiding?

I start to yawn.

Dad reads me
a story.

We say,
"I love you."